Fix and Mend

In these stories you will meet:

Spencer	Henry	James

Victor	Thomas	Kevin

The Fat Controller

And these more difficult words:

listen   loud   mean   talk   one

EGMONT

We bring stories to life

Book Band: Yellow

First published in Great Britain in 2016 by Egmont UK Limited,
The Yellow Building, 1 Nicholas Road, London W11 4AN

Thomas the Tank Engine & Friends™

CREATED BY BRITT ALLCROFT

Based on the Railway Series by the Reverend W Awdry
© 2016 Gullane (Thomas) LLC. Thomas the Tank Engine & Friends and
Thomas & Friends are trademarks of Gullane (Thomas) Limited.
Thomas the Tank Engine & Friends and Design is Reg. U.S. Pat. & Tm. Off.
© 2016 HIT Entertainment Limited.

HiT entertainment

ISBN 978 1 4052 8257 4

63401/1

Printed in Singapore

Stay safe online. Egmont is not responsible
for content hosted by third parties.

Series and book banding consultant: Nikki Gamble

Fix and Mend

This is Victor. Victor's job
is to fix and mend.

But Victor had jobs to do at the Docks so Thomas had to help Kevin.

Victor and Kevin told
Thomas what to do.
Thomas did not listen.

Spencer needed help.
He had a scratch on his paint.
Thomas did not listen.

Henry needed help.
His firebox needed cleaning.
Thomas did not listen.

James needed help. He had
twigs stuck in his funnel.
Thomas did
not listen.

Kevin wanted to help.
But he went too fast.
CRASH!

It was a big mess!
And then Victor
came back.

Victor was not happy.

Thomas you must listen.

Thomas did listen.
He did all the jobs.

Peep, peep Thomas!

Best Of All

This is Kevin. He helps Victor.

Kevin often drops things.

One day Kevin heard a big train rush past.
It was Spencer.
Spencer was very loud.

Spencer was mean to
Thomas and Gordon.
He told them he was
the best.

Spencer was mean
to Kevin.

He told him he
was the best.

SPENCER

The next day, Spencer went fast past Gordon. He tried to be mean and loud but he was not able to talk.

Spencer saw The Fat Controller but he was not able to talk.

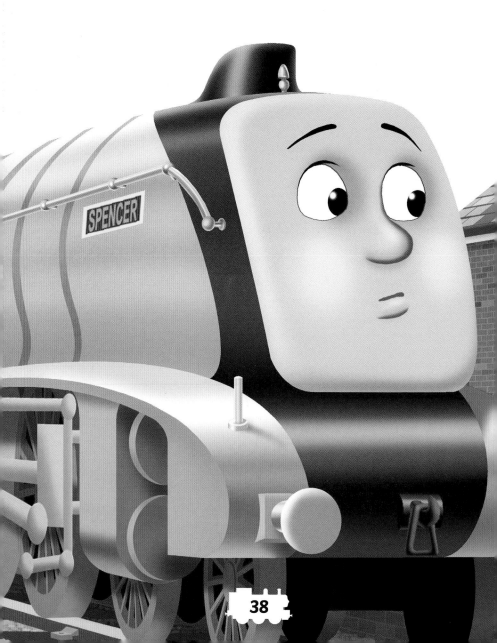

The sun set. Spencer
was still not able
to talk.

The next day Spencer was **still** not able to talk.

Spencer
needed help.

Kevin was happy to help Spencer. He mended him.

Spencer told the trains that Kevin was the best of all.

Clumsy Kevin

Kevin has dropped lots of things.
Read out loud what they are and
help him pick them up by following
your finger along the dotted trails.

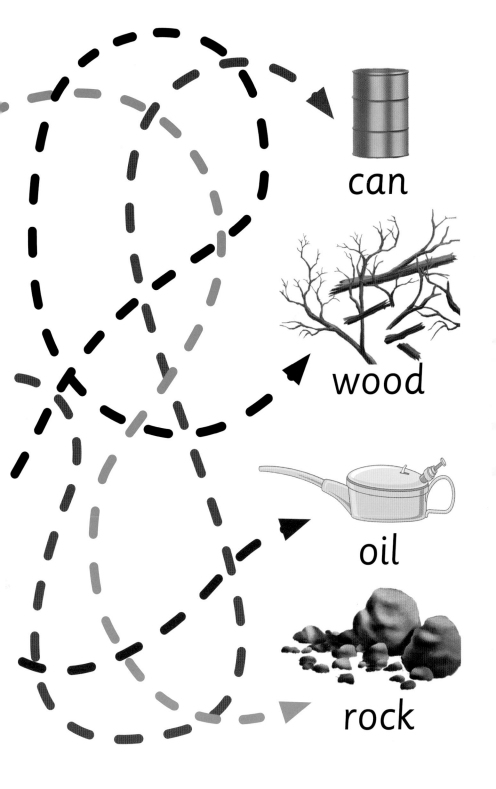

can

wood

oil

rock

Thomas Time

These words all start with the 't' sound.
Can you find them all in the picture?

Thomas   tracks

Toby   tree